THE KNACK

THE KNACK

A Comedy
by
ANN JELLICOE

FABER AND FABER
24 Russell Square
London

First published in mcmlxii
by Encore Publishing Company
This edition first published in mcmlxiv
by Faber and Faber Limited
24 Russell Square London W.C.1
Printed in Great Britain by
Latimer Trend & Co Ltd Plymouth

B − 3 MAY 1967

To
ROGER and KEITH

This play was first presented by The English Stage Company at the Arts Theatre, Cambridge on 9th October 1961 with the following cast:

Tom	Terry Palmer
Colin	Ronald Falk
Tolen	David Sumner
Nancy	Rita Tushingham

Directed by Keith Johnstone
Designed by Alan Tagg

It was subsequently produced in London at the Royal Court Theatre on 27th March 1962 with the following cast:

Tom	James Bolam
Colin	Philip Locke
Tolen	Julian Glover
Nancy	Rita Tushingham

Directed by Ann Jellicoe and Keith Johnstone
Designed by Alan Tagg

CHARACTERS

TOM : Smallish in size. Vigorous, balanced, strong and sensitive in his movements. He speaks with a great range of pitch, pace and volume and with immense energy and vitality.

COLIN : Tall and uncoordinated. Explodes into speech and talks jerkily, flatly, haltingly. Basically a strong and intelligent man, but unsure of himself. Gets very angry with himself.

TOLEN : Once an unpromising physical specimen he has developed himself by systematic physical exercise. His body is now much as he would like it to be. He appears strong, well-built, full of rippling muscle. All his movements are a conscious display of this body. He almost always speaks with a level, clipped smoothness and a very considered subtlety of tone.

NANCY : Aged about seventeen. Potentially a beautiful girl but her personality, like her appearance, is still blurred and unformed. She wears an accordion-pleated skirt.

The acting area should be as close to the audience as possible.

10

ACT ONE

A room. The room is in the course of being painted by
TOM. *The distribution of the paint is determined by the way
the light falls. There is a window up left in the back wall and
another down right. The paint is darkest where the shadows
are darkest and light where they are most light. The painting
is not smooth, pretty or finished, but fierce and determined.
Onstage there is a step-ladder, a divan, two simple wooden
chairs; a pair of chest expanders hangs from the door (down
left).*
Curtain up. TOM *onstage. Enter* COLIN.

COLIN: Er . . . I . . . er . . .

TOM: Fabulous. It's fabulous. It's fantastic.
(*Pause.*)

COLIN: Er . . .

TOM: Is it dry yet?

COLIN: Where?

TOM: Anywhere.
(COLIN *tries.*)

COLIN: Getting on.

TOM: Good.
(*Pause.*)

COLIN: I . . . er . . .

TOM: I hate that divan. (*Pause.*) More white there
perhaps. More white. (*Pause.*) Here. How does
the light fall?

11

COLIN: Eh?

TOM: The light. Get with it. White where it's light, black where it's dark, grey in between. (*Pause.*)

COLIN: Oh yes . . . yes.

TOM: Yes? Good. More white. (*He takes a brush of black paint and paints.*) Blast. (*He gets a rag, looks at wall, considers it and then starts working black paint with rag.*) Yes? Yes? (*Pause.*) Yes?

COLIN: It's not in the system.

TOM: Eh?

COLIN: White where it's light, black where it's dark.

TOM: It's nice. I like it.

COLIN: You're so messy. Everything's messed. It's so badly done.

TOM: I'm not, I'm not a decorator. It looks different, yes?

COLIN: Different?

TOM: Yes.

COLIN: To what?

TOM: To before I moved in. (*Pause.*) He won't like it.

COLIN: Who won't?

TOM: It'll annoy him. It'll annoy Tolen. It'll enrage him.

COLIN: The house doesn't belong to Tolen.

TOM: He'll say it's childish.

COLIN: It's my house. I rent it, so it's mine. (*Pause.*) There's a lot of stuff in the passage.

TOM: Ha ha! Because Tolen didn't think of it first.

COLIN: The passage is all bunged up. I want to bring my bed downstairs.

TOM: What's Tolen's first name?

COLIN: He says he hasn't got one.

TOM: Not got one?

12

COLIN: He never uses it. I want to bring my bed . . .
TOM: If he never uses it . . .
COLIN: . . . My bed downstairs.
TOM: He must have it.
COLIN: I want to bring my bed——
TOM: Well bring it down! What?
COLIN: I can't get it out of the front door.
TOM: You want to bring your bed——?
COLIN: There's too much stuff in the passage.
TOM: I put the stuff in the passage.
COLIN: There's a chest of drawers behind the front door. You can't get out.
TOM: Or in. Where's Tolen?
COLIN: Out. (*Pause.*) Seeing a girl.
TOM: Oh.
COLIN: There's too much stuff in the passage.
TOM: Why do you want to bring your bed downstairs?
COLIN: The wardrobe and the chest of drawers. We'll bring them in here.
TOM: What!
COLIN: Temporarily.
TOM: No.
COLIN: So I can get the bed through the front door.
TOM: We'll bring the bed in here and take it out through the window.
(*Slight pause.*)
COLIN: You only put the wardrobe outside while you were painting.
TOM: I don't want it back. The room's so beautiful.
COLIN: But you must be practical——
TOM: This blasted thing——
COLIN: You've got to sit——
TOM: The bottom's falling out.
COLIN: You've got to sleep——

13

TOM : Chairs!

COLIN : You can't sleep on the floor. Chairs?

TOM : On the floor. Sleep on it! I think I'll put the mattress on the floor!

COLIN : What!

TOM : Yes! The mattress on the floor. An empty—an empty beautiful room! What an angle! Look! Upwards? What an idea!
(COLIN *sinks bewildered on to a chair.*)
You marvel, you! (*Seizes* COLIN'*s chair.*) On the wall! Out of the way! Off the floor! I'll hang them on the wall!

COLIN : Oh no!

TOM : Oh yes! (*Throws mattress on floor.*) Help! You! Come on! Help me! Help me! Colin! My God, what a splendid idea!

COLIN : There's too much stuff in the passage.

TOM : Put it in the basement.

COLIN : We haven't got a basement.

TOM : Give it to Tolen! Put it in Tolen's room! Yes! Come on, help me! Oh! A beautiful empty room! Why do you want to bring your bed downstairs?

COLIN : Getting another.

TOM : Oh?

COLIN : A bigger one. Six foot.
(*Pause.*)

TOM : Let's get this shifted.

COLIN : Hadn't we better bring mine in first?

TOM : Into the basement. Give it to Tolen.
(*Noise, (off), of motor-bike which shudders to a stop outside the front door.*)

COLIN : We haven't got a basement.

TOM : Tolen. That's his motor-bike.

14

(*Sound of somebody trying front door.*)

COLIN: It's Tolen. He can't get in. (*Shouting.*) Be with you.

(*Exit* TOM *and* COLIN *with divan. Enter* TOLEN *through window upstage.* COLIN *appears at window and disappears.*)

COLIN: (*off*). Not there.

TOM: (*off*). What?

COLIN: (*off*). He's disappeared.

TOM: (*off*). That's odd.

(*Enter* TOM *through door followed by* COLIN.)

COLIN: Oh there you . . .

TOLEN: Your windows are rather dirty.

TOM: Let's wash them.

COLIN: I—I've got some Windolene.

(*Exit* COLIN.)

TOM: What's that?

COLIN: (*off*). For cleaning windows.

(*Pause. Re-enter* COLIN *with Windolene which he hands to* TOM.)

TOM: (*reading label*). Wipe it on Windolene,
Wipe it off window clean.

(TOM *wipes some of the Windolene on the bottom half of the window.*)

TOLEN: Washing with clean water and then polishing with newspaper would have less electro-static action.

COLIN: Oh?

TOLEN: Would repel dirt more efficiently.

(TOM *starts to experiment with the various shapes he can make.*)

TOLEN: Now you must do the top half, Tom.

(TOM *hoists the bottom half of the window up and*

15

crosses to window D.R. *and puts on the Windolene there*.)

TOLEN : You do realize, Tom, that in order to clean the window, you have to wipe off the Windolene? (*Pause*.) The white stuff has to be polished off the window.

TOM : Let's get that bed down, shall we, Colin?

COLIN : You can't leave that stuff on.

TOM : Oh?

TOLEN : You can't leave it on. "Wipe on sparingly with a damp cloth and wipe off immediately."

TOM : It's as good as net curtains, only better.

COLIN : Net curtains?

TOM : You should paint your windows white, Tolen. White reflects heat. You'll be O.K. when the bomb drops.
(*Exit* TOM.)

COLIN : What? What did you say?

TOM : (*off*). O.K. when the bomb drops. O.K. when the . . .

COLIN : Net curtains?
(*Exit* COLIN. *Pause*. TOLEN *is about to exit when he hears bumps, crashes and yells, off. This resolves into dialogue*):

COLIN : (*off*). It won't go round.

TOM : (*off*). It will.

COLIN : (*off*). It won't. Take it apart.

TOM : (*off*). What?

COLIN : (*off*). Take it to bits.

TOM : (*off*). Oh, all right.

COLIN : (*off*). Can you take the head?

TOM : (*off*). The what?

COLIN : (*off*). The head! Hold the head! The head!

TOM : (*off*). Help!

16

COLIN : (*off*). Eh?

TOM : (*off*). Help! Help!

COLIN : (*off*). Mind the plaster. (*Crash (off*).) Oh!

TOM : (*off*). You're so houseproud.

(*Enter* COLIN *with head of bed.* COLIN *is about to
lean head against wall.*)

Not where it's wet! Fool!

(COLIN *leans head against step-ladder. Crash
(off*).)

Help! Help! I'm stuck! (*Laughing.*) I'm stuck!
The foot!

COLIN : The what?

TOM : (*off*). The foot!

COLIN : Your foot!

(*Exit* COLIN.)

TOM : (*off*). Of the bed.

(*Banging and crashing (off*) *with various
imprecations. Enter* COLIN *with foot of bed.*)

TOLEN : Have there been any telephone calls?

COLIN : Eh?

TOLEN : I'm expecting a couple of girls to telephone.

COLIN : There was a Maureen and er—a Joan.

TOLEN : Joan? Joan who?

(COLIN *is nonplussed.*)

Never mind, she'll telephone again. (*Pause.*) I
was afraid it was the barmaid at the "Sun".

COLIN : Alice?

(*Enter* TOM.)

TOLEN : She took me into the little back room this
morning.

TOM : What about Jimmy?

TOLEN : Probably at Chapel.

TOM : On Saturday?

TOLEN : She said he was at Chapel. Beyond that bead

curtain you know, there's a room full of silver cups. Cases of them. And a large pink sofa in the middle. I never knew Jimmy was a sporting man.

COLIN: Who was the other one?

TOLEN: The other?

COLIN: The one you were expecting to telephone.

TOLEN: Girl I met in a telephone kiosk.

(*Exit* TOLEN. *Small crash* (*off*). *Re-enter* TOLEN.)

TOLEN: Colin, would you mind moving that bed? I would like to get up to my room.

COLIN: Oh, the base. Sorry.

TOM: Can't you climb over?

(*Exit* COLIN. *Crashing sounds* (*off*). *Re-enter* COLIN.)

COLIN: (*to* TOM). Give me a hand, will you?

TOM: Why can't Tolen?

COLIN: Eh?

TOM: It's him that wants to get upstairs.

COLIN: Oh, er . . .

(*Exit* COLIN. *Re-enter dragging base.*)

TOM: Mind the paint.

(TOM *helps* COLIN *onstage with bed.*)

TOLEN: Why are you bringing your bed downstairs, Colin?

COLIN: Getting a new one.

TOLEN: Oh?

COLIN: A bigger one—six foot.

TOLEN: Oh, like mine.

COLIN: I—er—I thought—I thought I'd like another one. You know—er—bigger. Just—just in case, you know. I thought I'd like a bigger—another bed—more comfortable. (*Pause.*) I could always put my married cousins up.

18

(*Long pause.*)

TOLEN: Have you got a girl yet, Colin?

COLIN: No.

TOLEN: Carol left six months ago, didn't she?

COLIN: Mm.

TOM: Have you got a girl yet, Colin?

COLIN: No.

TOM: Got a woman?

COLIN: No.

TOM: You haven't, have you.

COLIN: No.

TOM: You haven't!

COLIN: No.

TOM: You haven't! You haven't! You fool! Why d'you want another bed?

COLIN: Mind my bed!

TOM: His bed! Colin's bed!

COLIN: It's not strong.

TOM: (*through the bars*). Grr! Grr!

COLIN: Hey! Stop! Stop it!

TOM: It creaks! It runs! It spins! Watch it! Yahoo!

COLIN: You'll——

TOM: Poop—poop——

COLIN: I say——

TOM: Poop poop poop poop——

COLIN: Stop it. Stop it.

TOM: Poop poop, look out!

COLIN: Stop stop—ow!

(*Everything collapses.* TOM *and* COLIN *are enmeshed in the bed and step-ladder.*)

COLIN: You—you—you nit.

(*Pause.*)

TOLEN: Did you put turpentine in the white?

TOM: Eh?

19

TOLEN : The white paint. Did you put turpentine in the white?

TOM : Yes.

TOLEN : It'll go yellow.

COLIN : What?

TOLEN : The white paint will go yellow. ·

COLIN : Yellow!

TOLEN : Yes.

COLIN : I never knew that.

TOLEN : The turpentine thins the white lead in the paint and the linseed oil seeps through and turns the white yellow.

COLIN : Oh. D'you think we should do it again?

(TOM *is pulling at the chest expanders*.)

TOM : Peter left these, wasn't it nice of him?

(*Pause. A girl passes the window.* TOLEN *starts to exit through window*.)

COLIN : Where you going? Where——

(*Exit* TOLEN.)

How does he do it?

TOM : He's beginning to wear out my window. Let's move the chest of drawers so he can come in through the front door. He doesn't actually do them in the street, you know.

COLIN : Doesn't he?

TOM : He makes his contact and stashes them up for later. He's enlarging his collection.

COLIN : How does he meet them?

TOM : Your bed's in the way. What are we going to do with this bed? What you going to do with it?

COLIN : Oh that. Oh—what's the use?

(TOM *lugs part of the bed across and leans it against* COLIN.)

What's Tolen got that I haven't got? Maureen

20

says Tolen's got sexy ankles.

(TOM *brings up another piece and leans it against* COLIN.)

Are my ankles sexy?

TOM: What are you going to do with this bed?

COLIN: Thought I'd take it round to Copp Street.

TOM: Copp Street?

COLIN: To the junk yard.

TOM: To sell?

COLIN: I thought so.

TOM: For money?

COLIN: Why not? Why——

TOM: Don't move!

COLIN: Why not?

TOM: It'll fall. (*Pause.*) O.K. We'll take it round to Copp Street. How far is it to Copp Street?

COLIN: Twenty minutes.

TOM: Twenty! (*Long pause.*) Put it back in your room. (*Pause.* COLIN *shakes his head. Pause.* TOM *opens his mouth to speak.*)

COLIN: (*interrupting*). Not in the passage. (*Pause.*)

TOM: Can't you just stand there? You look quite nice really.
(*Slight pause.*)

COLIN: Put it together.

TOM: No.

COLIN: If we put it together it'll stand by itself.

TOM: No.

COLIN: On its own feet.

TOM: I can't bear it.
(*Pause.*)

COLIN: Take the foot.
(TOM *does so listlessly.*)

21

And the head.
(TOM *does so*.)

TOM: How can you sleep on this? I'd think I was at the zoo.

COLIN: How d'you get a woman? How can I get a girl? (*They start to put the bed together*.)

TOM: Do you know why the Duck-billed Platypus can't be exported from Australia—or do I mean platipi?

COLIN: How can I get a woman?

TOM: You think this is going to be a silly story, don't you.

COLIN: Well?

TOM: Because they eat their own weight in worms every day and they starve to death in one and a half hours or something. It's rather a nice object. It's not a nice bed but it's not a bad object. Yes. Look. It's rather nice.
(COLIN *picks up mattress*.)
No.

COLIN: But——

TOM: No.

COLIN: But a mattress naturally goes on a bed.

TOM: It's not a bed. It's an object. More than that, it's wheeled traffic. Mm. Not much room, is there? I must get those chairs off the floor. Put the mattress in the passage.

COLIN: It's more comfy on the bed.

TOM: Oh, very well.
(TOM *experiments with the bed*.)

COLIN: Why is Tolen so sexy?
(TOLEN *passes the window and tries the front door. Enters by window*.)

TOM: You were very quick. Did she repulse you?

22

TOLEN : No. I'm seeing her later.

TOM : Next time I'll time you.

TOLEN : Next time come and watch me.

(TOM *takes the chest expanders and tries them a few times.*)

TOM : I'm getting pretty good. Whew! I can do ten of these. Whew! It's awful!

TOLEN : I can do twenty—but then . . .

TOM : Let's see you.

(TOLEN *indicates he is below bothering to use his energy.*)

COLIN : I can do twenty as well.

TOM : Let's see you.

(COLIN *takes the chest expanders and starts.*)

He's bending his elbows, it's easier that way.

COLIN : Four.

TOM : Tolen.

TOLEN : Yes, Tom?

TOM : Do you think it's a good idea for Colin to buy a six-foot bed?

TOLEN : Where's he buying it?

COLIN : Nine. (*Pause.*) Catesby's.

TOM : Plutocrat.

TOLEN : Heal's would have been better.

COLIN : Twelve. Eh?

TOLEN : Heal's have more experience with beds.

COLIN : Expensive. Fourteen.

TOLEN : They may be more expensive, but they have more experience. You pay for their greater experience.

TOM : Yes, but do you think it's a good idea, a sound idea, ethically, for Colin to buy a six-foot bed when he hasn't got a woman?

TOLEN : Rory McBride has a six-foot bed.

TOM: Don't stop! You have to keep it up the whole time. You're not allowed to stop. How sexy is Rory McBride? Who is he anyway?

COLIN: D'you think——?

TOM: Don't stop!

COLIN: D'you think——?

TOM: What?

COLIN: I ought to get a six-foot bed?
(COLIN *stops*.)

TOM: How many?

COLIN: Twenty-four. (*Staggering*.) Where's the bed?

TOM: You mean the object.
(COLIN *collapses on the bed. A girl is seen to pass the window. Exit* TOLEN *through window*.)

COLIN: Where's he gone?

TOM: A girl passed by and he went after her.
(*Pause*.)

COLIN: You got a cigarette?

TOM: I thought you didn't smoke.

COLIN: Have you got a cigarette?

TOM: No. (*Pause*.) Listen, Colin, I've had a new idea for you. For teaching children about music.

COLIN: Oh——

TOM: Listen! My idea about the chalk—was it a good one?

COLIN: It was all right.

TOM: Did you use it or not? Did you?

COLIN: All right. All right. Just tell me.

TOM: Tolen could help, blast him.

COLIN: How?

TOM: He's a musician. You need his advice. But don't let that bastard near the kids, he'll bully them. Now listen, I been thinking about this. You got a piano? Well, have you? Golly the bleeding

24

school wouldn't be furnished without a piano.

COLIN: We've got one.

TOM: Good. Listen, I been thinking about this.
Teaching's so intellectual and when it's not
intellectual, it's bossy, or most of it. The
teachers tell the kids everything and all they get
is dull little copycats, little automata; dim,
limited and safe——

COLIN: Oh, get on.

TOM: You get the piano and you get the kids and you
say it's a game see? "Right," you say, "You're
not to look at the keys, 'cos that's cheating."

COLIN: Not look——

TOM: If they look at each other playing, they'll just
copy each other. Now, don't put your own
brain between them and the direct experience.
Don't intellectualize. Let them come right up
against it. And don't talk about music, talk
about noise.

COLIN: Noi——

TOM: What else is music but an arrangement of
noises? I'm serious. "Now," you say, "one of
you come out here and make noises on the
piano." And finally one of them will come out
and sort of hit the keys, bang, bang. "Right,"
you say, "now someone come out and make the
same noise."

COLIN: Eh?

TOM: The same noise. That's the first step. They'll
have to *listen* to see they hit in the same place—
and they can do it more or less 'cos they can
sort of—you know—clout it in the middle bit.
So next you get them all going round the piano
in a circle, all making the same noise, and

they'll love that. When they get a bit cheesed,
you develop it. "O.K.," you say, "let's have
another noise."

COLIN: I don't see the point, I mean——

TOM: Now listen, this way they'll find out for
themselves, give them a direct experience and
they'll discover for themselves—all the basic
principles of music and they won't shy away—
they won't think of it as culture, it'll be pop to
them. Listen! You, goon, moron, you don't like
Bartok, do you?

COLIN: No.

TOM: Don't be so pleased with yourself. You don't
understand it, your ear's full of Bach, it stops at
Mahler. But after a few lessons like this, you
play those kids Schoenberg, you play them
Bartok. They'll know what he's doing. I bet
they will! It'll be rock'n roll to them. My God,
I ought to be a teacher! My God I'm a genius!

COLIN: What about Tolen?

TOM: What about him?

COLIN: You said he could help.

TOM: To borrow his gramophone records.

COLIN: He never lends them, he never lets anyone else
touch them. (*Pause.*) It's a good idea.

TOM: Good.

COLIN: Thanks. (*Pause.*) Why do you say Tolen is a
bastard?

TOM: Be careful. He only dazzles you for one reason.
Really, Colin, sex, sex, sex: that's all we ever
get from you.

COLIN: It's all right for you and Tolen.

TOM: We're all of us more or less total sexual failures.

COLIN: Tolen isn't a sexual failure.

26

TOM: He needs it five hours a day, he says.

COLIN: Then he can't be a sexual failure. (*Pause.*) He can't be a sexual failure. (*Pause.*) He can't be a sexual failure having it five hours a day. (*Pause.*) Can he?

(*Long pause.*)

TOM: I don't like that wall. There's something wrong with that wall. It's not right.

COLIN: Can he?

(NANCY *appears outside behind the window up left and looks about her.*)

TOM: Hm. Colin——

COLIN: Can he?

TOM: Colin.

(NANCY *vanishes.*)

COLIN: What?

TOM: Oh nothing. What do you think about that wall?

COLIN: Blast the wall! Blast the bloody wall!

TOM: Don't shout.

COLIN: I'm not shouting.

TOM: You're not listening.

(NANCY *reappears outside the window.*)

COLIN: Oh . . . oh . . . oh . . .

TOM: Speak to her.

COLIN: I—I——

TOM: Ask her the time. Ask her to lend you sixpence.

COLIN: I—I—you.

TOM: Eh?

COLIN: You—please.

TOM: I can't do it for you.

COLIN: Oh——

(COLIN *turns away. Pause.* NANCY *vanishes. Long pause.*)

TOM: What do you think about that wall?

COLIN: What? Oh . . . it's . . . it's . . .

(COLIN *does something violent. Pause. Enter* TOLEN *through window.*)

TOM: Someone was riding your motor-bike.

TOLEN: What?

(*Exit* TOLEN *through window.*)

COLIN: Who was riding his motor-bike?

(*Re-enter* TOLEN *through window.*)

TOM: I swear someone was riding your motor-bike. (*Pause.*) Well?

TOLEN: Well?

TOM: How long did you take this time?

TOLEN: Did you time me?

TOM: Did you time yourself?

COLIN: How long did you take?

TOLEN: Not more than about ten minutes——

COLIN: Ten minutes! Only ten minutes!

TOLEN: Really, Colin, do you think I'm so clumsy, so vulgar as to do it in the street? I'm meeting her . . .

TOM: Ten minutes! Ten minutes from door to door? From start to finish? From hello to good-bye?

COLIN: Ten minutes.

TOM: Ten Tolen! Ten! Ten minutes! Ten whole minutes! What! No! You're slipping, man! You're sliding! You're letting us down! Ten. You can do better than that. Faster man! Faster! Faster! Faster!

COLIN: Eh?

TOM: Give him a drink of water. Listen, Tolen. Three! Three! Three! D'you hear? Dreams I got for you, Tolen. Dreams and plans I got for you. Four minutes! Get it down to four minutes.

28

Four minutes from start to finish—like the
four-minute mile.

COLIN: Eh?

TOM: Heroic! Think! A new series in the Olympic
Games!

COLIN: Is he joking?

TOM: And then, Tolen, by discipline, by training, by
application: three minutes fifty-nine seconds!
Three minutes fifty-five! Three minutes fifty!
And then—one day—one unimaginable day:
three minutes! Three minutes from start to
finish!

COLIN: Is it nicer, faster?

TOM: Nice? Nice? Nice? That's not the point. My
God! I'm disappointed in you, Tolen, My God
I am! Yes! I am! A man with every advantage,
every opportunity, every accoutrement—God's
gift to woman! And think of those women
Tolen: waiting to be satisfied—their need,
Tolen, their crying need—(*weeping*.) And with
the capacity, with the capacity for, with the
capacity for spreading yourself around.
(*Pause while* TOM *regains control*.)

TOLEN: I think you're mad.

TOM: Ah, Tolen, never mind. Relax. I see what you
mean. I'm a man too. I understand. Yes, I do.
Yes, yes I do. (*Slight pause*.) You couldn't do it.
(*Slight pause*.) You couldn't keep it up. You
couldn't keep up the pace.
(TOLEN *appears slightly restive*.)
Nobody could. It's too much. It's too fast. It's
not human, it's superhuman. No, no, let's forget
it. Let's be generous. I understand. (*Pause*.)
Wait! Here's what I propose. Here's what I

suggest. One in three! One in three in your own
time! Yes Tolen, every third one as long as you
like.

(TOLEN *yawns and climbs on the bed.*)

He's tired. He's weary. He's overdone it. Poor
chap. He's tired. Poor bloke. Quick, quick.
Blankets! Brandy! Pills! Pillows! Nurses!
Stretchers! Doses! Nurses! Horlicks! Nurses!
Hot water bottles! Nurses! Nurses! Nurses!
Nurses! Have a piece of barley sugar.

(NANCY *appears at window.* TOLEN *takes notice.*
NANCY *disappears.*)

Save yourself! Control yourself! Give yourself a
chance!

TOLEN: A bit too provincial.

COLIN: What?

TOLEN: That girl.

(*Pause.*)

TOM: (*really wanting to know*). How can you tell she's
provincial?

TOLEN: Of course, Tom, you will not appreciate that the
whole skill, the whole science, is in the slowness:
the length of time a man may take. The skill is
in the slowness. Of course, Tom, I don't expect
you can appreciate this. There is little skill,
Tom, and no subtlety in the three-minute make.
However——

COLIN: It's better slower?

TOLEN: However, if I wished, Tom, if I wanted, you do
realize that I could do it in about eighty-five
seconds.

TOM: Yes.

COLIN: Tolen.

TOLEN: Yes, Colin?

30

COLIN: Will you—I mean—will you show me— (*pause*) how— (*pause*)?

TOLEN: You mean how I get women?

COLIN: Yes.

TOLEN: I can tell you what I know intellectually, Colin, what my experience has been. But beyond that it's a question of intuition. Intuition is, to some degree, inborn, Colin. One is born with an intuition as to how to get women. But this feeling can be developed with experience and confidence, in certain people, Colin, to some degree. A man can develop the knack.
(*Pause.*)
First you must realize that women are not individuals but types. No, not even types, just women. They want to surrender but they don't want the responsibility of surrendering. This is one reason why the man must dominate.
On the other hand there are no set rules. A man must be infinitely subtle; must use his intuition, a very subtle intuition. If you feel it necessary in order to get the woman you must even be prepared to humiliate yourself, to grovel, to utterly abase yourself before the woman—I mean only in cases of extreme necessity, Colin. After all, what does it matter? It's just part of getting her. Once you've got her it's the woman that grovels. Finally, Colin, the man is the master.
For you must appreciate, Colin, that people like to be dominated. They like to be mastered. They ask to be relieved of the responsibility of deciding for themselves. It's a kindness towards people to relieve them of responsibility. In this

31

world, Colin, there are the masters and there
are the servants. Very few men are real men,
Colin, are real masters. Almost all women are
servants. They don't want to think for themselves, they want to be dominated.
First you must establish contact. Of course you
won't find that as easy as I do. I'm not referring
to touch, tactile communication, that comes
later. I mean the feeling between you. You are
aware of the girl, the girl is aware of you, a
vibration between you . . .

COLIN: Just a minute.

TOLEN: Yes?

COLIN: I just want to get it straight.

TOLEN: Take your time.

(*Pause.*)

COLIN: I don't see what you mean by contact.

TOLEN: Very difficult to explain. Tom, can you explain?

TOM: No.

TOLEN: Once you feel it, Colin, you will know it next
time. Having established this basis of contact,
then you work to break down her resistance, to
encourage surrender. Flattery is useful; if a
woman is intelligent make her think she's pretty,
if she's pretty make her think she's beautiful.
Never let them think, never let them see you are
clever or intellectual. Never be serious with a
woman. Once you let a woman start thinking,
the whole process takes infinitely more time.
Keep her laughing, keep her talking; you can
judge by her laughter, by the way she laughs,
how you're getting on.
Perhaps it might be useful to consider what is
the right food.

COLIN: The right food?

TOLEN: Food is of the utmost importance. Food is of the essence. One's body needs protein and energy-giving substance. I find with my perhaps unusual sexual demands that my body requires at least twice the normal daily intake of protein.

COLIN: Protein?

TOLEN: Cheese, eggs, milk, meat. I drink about four pints of milk a day—Channel Island milk. And eat about a pound of steak. It needn't be the most expensive, the cheaper cuts have the same food value. For instance, skirt.

TOM: Skirt?

TOLEN: Skirt.

COLIN: Skirt. Cheese, eggs, milk, meat, skirt. Got a pencil, Tom.

TOLEN: Skirt is meat.

COLIN: Oh.

TOM: Don't you see what you're doing to this growing lad? He hasn't got a woman, now he'll go and eat himself silly on milk and meat. Stoke up the fire and block up the chimney. Listen, Colin, suppose this was a piano.

TOLEN: A what?

COLIN: Shut up.

TOM: A piano. Plonk, plonk, plonk.

TOLEN: It's a bed.

TOM: It's not, it's a piano, listen.

COLIN: I want Tolen to tell me——

TOM: Shut up, he's told you enough. A piano, plonk. Now supposing you couldn't——

COLIN: Listen, Tolen——

TOM: Supposing you couldn't see my hand——

COLIN: Shut up.

TOM: I play—C sharp, F and A——
COLIN: Tolen——
(NANCY *passes window*.)
I want—listen to me. I want to hear what—I want to hear what Tolen has to say. Listen—listen to me. I want to hear wh-what Tolen has to say. So *what* you think it's b-bad for me to listen to Tolen. You're not in charge of me. I am and I'm sick of myself, I'm absolutely sick, and here I am stuck with myself. I want to hear what Tolen has to say——
(NANCY *reappears at window*.)
I want to hear what Tolen has to say. So *what* I want to hear, I want to hear what——
(NANCY *taps at window. Pause*.)
NANCY: Do you know where I can find the Y.W.C.A.?
(*Pause*.)
TOM: The what?
NANCY: The Y.W.C.A.
(*Pause*.)
TOM: Come on in. Come in by the front door.
(*Exit* TOM.)
NANCY: Oh thanks. Thanks very much.
(*Sound of weighty object being moved. Enter* NANCY *carrying a holdall and a carrier bag and* TOM *carrying a large suitcase*.)
NANCY: Hullo.
TOLEN: Hullo.
NANCY: Hullo.
COLIN: Oh, hullo.
(*Pause*.)
TOM: Well, has anyone seen it?
COLIN: Seen what?
TOM: Seen what?

34

NANCY: The Y.W.C.A.

TOM: The Y.W.C.A.

COLIN: Oh, the Y.W.C.A.

TOM: Yes.

COLIN: No.
(*Pause.*)

TOM: Would you like to sit down?

NANCY: Well, thanks, but—but well, thanks.
(*She sits.*)

TOM: Would you like a cup of tea or something?

NANCY: Oh, well, no thanks, really.

TOM: No trouble, it's no trouble. I'll put the kettle on
(*Exit* TOM.)

TOLEN: Did he say he'd put a kettle on? He's not boiled
a kettle since he came here.

TOM: (*off*). Colin!

COLIN: Yes?

TOM: (*off*). How do you turn the gas on?
(*Pause.* TOLEN *now pursues the intention of
teasing* NANCY *and making her uncomfortable.
He succeeds. If possible achieve this without
words. But if necessary insert line:*
TOLEN: "*Bit short in the neck. Nice hair though.*"
Enter TOM.)

TOM: How do you turn— (*pause.*) What do you think
of our piano?

NANCY: What?

TOM: Our piano: Do you like it? Our piano?

NANCY: What piano?

TOM: This piano.

NANCY: Piano?

TOM: Yes.

NANCY: That's not a piano.

TOM: Yes it is, it's a piano.

35

NANCY: It's a bed.

TOM: It's a piano, honest, listen: ping!

NANCY: It's a bed.

TOM: It's a piano, isn't it, Colin?

COLIN: Eh?

TOM: This is a piano.

COLIN: Piano?

TOM: Piano.

COLIN: Oh yes, a piano. Ping.

NANCY: It's a bed.

TOM: (*using the edge of the bed as keyboard*). Ping (*high*) ping (*low*). Ping (*running his finger right down: glissando*) pi-i-i-i-ng.

COLIN: (*middle*). Ping.

NANCY: It's a bed.

TOM: Bechstein.

NANCY: Bechstein?

TOM: (*high*) ping. (*Medium high*) ping. (*Medium low*) ping. (*Low*) ping.

NANCY: It's a bed.

TOM: (*1st 3 bars "Blue Danube" starting low*).
Ping ping ping ping ping.

NANCY: It's a bed.

COLIN: Rosewood.

TOM: (*4th and 5th bars B.D.*).
Ping ping
Ping ping.

NANCY: It's a bed.

TOM: (*6th, 7th, 8th bars B.D.*).
Ping ping ping ping ping
Ping ping.

COLIN: (*taking over 9th bar*). Ping ping.

TOM, COLIN: (*together playing chords in unison 10th–13th bars*).

Ping ping ping ping ping
Ping ping
Ping ping
Ping ping ping ping ping
Ping ping.

NANCY: (*tentative, taking over*). Ping ping.
TOM, COLIN: (*gently encouraging* NANCY *who joins in
17th, 18th, 19th bars B.D.*).
Ping ping ping ping ping
Ping ping
Ping ping.
(*All three letting go with great rich chords.*)
Ping ping ping ping ping
Ping ping
Ping ping
Ping ping ping ping ping
Ping ping ping ping
Ping ping ping ping ping ping.

NANCY: Ping.
COLIN: Ping.
NANCY: Ping.
COLIN: Ping.
NANCY: Ping.
COLIN: Plong.
NANCY: Plong.
COLIN: Plong plong.
NANCY: Ping plong.
COLIN: Plong.
NANCY: Ping.
COLIN: Ping.
NANCY: Plong.
(*Pause.*)
COLIN: Plong.
(*Pause.*)

NANCY: Plong.
    (*Pause.*)
COLIN: Plong.
TOLEN: Why be so childish about a bed?

> *Author's Note:* All the above could be rearranged or improvised to suit different actors and different productions provided the sequence of events is clear:
> 1. TOM and COLIN charm NANCY into entering into the game.
> 2. TOM retires leaving COLIN and NANCY getting on rather well, a growing relationship which TOLEN interrupts.

(*Long pause.*)

TOM: Would anyone like to know how they train lions to stand on boxes? (*Pause.*) Would you like to know how they train lions to stand on boxes? First we must have a box (*taking bucket*) That will do. Now this marks the limit of the cage—the edge, the bars.

TOLEN: Must you be so childish?

TOM: Childlike. The trainer takes his whip. Whip? Whip? We'll do without a whip. Now a lion. I must have a lion . . . Tolen, you'd make a good lion. No? O.K. Colin.

COLIN: No.

TOM: Come on, be a lion.

COLIN: No.

TOM: Go on, can't you roar? The trainer taking the box in his left hand, and the whip—imagine the whip—in his right, advances on the lion and drives him backward against the cage bars, yes? Now. There is a critical moment when the lion must leap at the attacker otherwise it will be too

38

late, see? Right. The trainer can recognize the critical moment. So, at the moment when the lion rears to attack, the trainer draws back and the lion, no longer threatened, drops his forepaws and finds himself standing on the box. Do this a few times and you've trained a lion to stand on a box.

(*Pause.*)

COLIN : How does the box get there?

TOM : What?

COLIN : You've still got it in your hand.

TOM : The trainer puts it there.

COLIN : When?

(*Pause.*)

TOM : Let's try. You come and be lion.

COLIN : No.

TOM : All right, I'll be lion. (*He tries a roar or two.*) Whew! It makes you feel sexy. (*He tries again.*)

COLIN : I'd like to be lion.

TOM : All right.

COLIN : I wonder if I could roar into something.

TOM : Eh?

COLIN : It would help the resonance. (*He roars into bucket.*)

TOM : That's the lion's box.

COLIN : Sounds marvellous inside.

(COLIN *sees* NANCY's *carrier bag. He picks it up.*)

TOM : Hey, you can't touch that.

COLIN : Eh?

NANCY : Oh, that's all right.

(COLIN *empties contents, including a copy of* Honey *magazine. Puts carrier bag on his head and goes round roaring.*)

TOM : Yes! Yes! Yes! Yes! Yes!

39

(COLIN *roars at* TOM *who roars back, then at*
NANCY. NANCY *laughs, half scared, half excited.*
COLIN *roars at her and she runs away.* COLIN
gropes around for her, but she evades him,
laughing.)

TOM: You should wear a carrier bag more often.

COLIN: Just a minute.

(COLIN *takes the bag off his head and makes holes*
for eyes. Replaces bag. Roars again after NANCY.
TOLEN *takes off belt he wears and cracks it like a*
whip.)

TOLEN: I'll be trainer.

TOM: Eh? Very well.

TOLEN: Ready?

(*Pause.* TOLEN *advances on* COLIN *cracking his*
"whip" and getting a sweet pleasure from the
identification. COLIN *roars,* TOLEN *gets more*
excited.)

TOLEN: Back—back you—back you—back—back you
beast you—beast you beast you back back!

(NANCY *gets mixed up between them. She screams*
and exits. TOLEN *picks up* Honey. *Pause.*)

TOM: Just think what you could do with a real whip,
Tolen. Or a Sjambok. Think of that.

COLIN: (*taking off carrier bag*). What's happened? Has
she gone?

TOM: She left her suitcases.

(*End of Act One*)

40

ACT TWO

The room is very peaceful. TOM *is painting gently and thinking about his paint.* COLIN *has the carrier bag on his head and is feeling free and experimental. Anything the actor may improvise is probably best, but* COLIN *might feel like some exotic bird: standing on one leg, hopping, crowing; possibly using the chest expanders in some unconventional way. After a long pause.*

TOM: What do you think?
    (*Pause.*)
COLIN: Not thinking.
    (*Pause.*)
TOM: Eh?
    (*Pause.*)
COLIN: Not thinking.
TOM: Look!
COLIN: Oh.
TOM: A . . . (*pause*). This place soothes me.
    (*Pause.* COLIN *takes off the carrier bag.*)
COLIN: I remember the first time I saw this street.
TOM: Northam Street?
COLIN: These mean streets (*pause*)—the feeling of space in these streets—it's fantastic. (*Pause.*) When they're empty they're sort of—splendid, a sort of—crumbling splendour (*pause*) and a feeling of—in winter, on a hazy, winter day a—a—a

41

——romantic! And in summer hot and—listless.
And at week-ends, summer and the sun shining
and children dashing about and mothers talking
—you know, gossiping and men cleaning motor-
bikes and (*getting excited*) they can be forbid-
ding, threatening—I mean—you know—if the
light's flat and darkish,—no sun—just flat and
lowering, it's stupendous! And early morning—
early autumn—I've walked through these streets
all alone, you know, all by myself—so quiet
so . . . so . . .

(*Telephone rings (off).*)

It'll be for him. It'll be for Tolen.

(COLIN *replaces carrier bag on his head and picks
up a magazine. Exit* TOM. *Telephone stops
ringing. Pause.* NANCY *appears at the window, she
doesn't see* COLIN. NANCY *climbs through the
window and goes towards the suitcases.* COLIN
sees NANCY. NANCY *sees* COLIN *and is transfixed.
Pause. Enter* TOLEN *through window. Pause.*
TOLEN *whips off his belt.* NANCY *darts away
hysterical. There is a maelstrom of movement
during which the bed gets overturned,* NANCY *is
caught behind it and* COLIN *and* TOLEN *are
covering all the exits. Enter* TOM *through door.
Pause.*)

TOM : Colin, take that carrier bag off your head.

COLIN : Eh?

TOM : Take it off.

(COLIN *removes carrier bag.*)

Shall we get the bed straight? (TOM *goes to the
foot of the bed.*) Tolen?

(TOM *and* COLIN *put bed right.*)

You not found the Y.W.C.A.?

42

NANCY: No.

TOM: What's the address?

NANCY: I've got it here. (*She hands him a scrap of paper.*)

TOM: Martin's Grove W.2. Where's Martin's Grove?

COLIN: I don't know. I'll get the street map.
(*Exit* COLIN. *Pause.*)

NANCY: Thanks.

TOLEN: That's all right.

NANCY: Oh, thanks.

TOLEN: Don't mention it.
(*Enter* COLIN *with map.*)

TOM: How does it work?

COLIN: Index.

TOM: Eh?

COLIN: Back.

TOM: I see.

TOLEN: Just come off the train, have you?

NANCY: Yes.

COLIN: James Park, James Square, turn over, and again.
Ah. Mapperton, Marlow.

TOLEN: Is it the——

TOM: Martin's Grove W.2. J4.73. What's that?

COLIN: Page seventy-three.

TOLEN: Is it the first time you've been here?

NANCY: Here?

TOLEN: In London?

NANCY: Oh yes.
(TOLEN *and* NANCY *laugh.*)

COLIN: Square J above, 4 across.

TOM: What tiny print.

TOLEN: You've got Chinese eyebrows.

NANCY: Eh?

TOLEN: Chinese eyebrows. Very clear arch. Very delicate.

NANCY: Have I?

TOLEN: Have you got a mirror, I'll show you.

NANCY: Oh.

COLIN: Turn it the other way.

TOM: Eh?

COLIN: Round. That's it.

TOLEN: See? Very pretty.

NANCY: Oh.

TOM: Here. (*Pause.*) Here it is.

NANCY: Eh? Oh, thanks.

TOM: Not far. Five minutes. (NANCY *is occupied with* TOLEN.) We'll take you. We'll take you there.

NANCY: Oh. Oh thanks. (*Pause.*) Well perhaps I ought to——

TOLEN: What's your name?

NANCY: Nancy, Nancy Jones. What's yours?

TOLEN: Tolen.

NANCY: Tolen? Tolen what?

TOLEN: Tolen.

NANCY: Tolen, oh I see, like Yana.

TOLEN: I beg your pardon?

NANCY: Yana.

TOLEN: Yana?

NANCY: Like Yana. Nothing Yana, Yana nothing.

TOLEN: Please would you tell me what you mean?

NANCY: You not heard her? She's a singer. She sings.

TOLEN: On television?

NANCY: And the radio. Is it your christian name or your surname? (*Pause.*) Well, is it? Is it your surname or your christian name?

TOLEN: It's my surname.

NANCY: What's your christian name?

TOLEN: I never use my first name. I have no first name.

NANCY: What is it?

TOLEN: I prefer not to use it.

44

NANCY: Why?

TOLEN: I don't use it. I have no first name. I never use my first name.

(TOLEN *moves away. Pause.* TOLEN *returns to near* NANCY. NANCY *shifts uncomfortably.*)

What's the matter? Is anything wrong? Is anything the matter with you?

NANCY: No.

TOLEN: Why are you so nervous?

NANCY: I'm not.

TOLEN: You look nervous.

NANCY: Me nervous? Do I?

TOLEN: Yes.

NANCY: Oh——

TOLEN: Yes?

NANCY: Nothing.

TOLEN: What's the matter?

NANCY: It's—it's——

TOLEN: Well?

NANCY: It's——

TOLEN: You are nervous, aren't you? Very nervous. Why don't you take your coat off?

NANCY: I don't want to.

TOLEN: My dear, you take it off.

NANCY: I don't want to.

TOLEN: Why don't you want to?

NANCY: No.

(*Exit* COLIN.)

It's—it's——

TOLEN: Yes?

(*Pause.*)

NANCY: You're looking at me.

TOLEN: Am I?

NANCY: Yes.

45

TOLEN: How am I looking?

NANCY: I don't know, I——

TOLEN: How am I looking?

NANCY: I——

TOLEN: Well?

NANCY: I feel——

TOLEN: What?

NANCY: I don't know, I——

TOLEN: You feel funny, don't you—go on, tell me—go on—tell me—tell me.

(NANCY *moves away*. TOLEN *laughs*.)

TOM: What's the most frightening building in London?

TOLEN: It depends what you mean by frightening.

TOM: Break it up, Tolen.

TOLEN: What I do is my affair, not yours.

TOM: She doesn't know a thing.

TOLEN: She knows what she wants, or rather what she will want.

TOM: I don't think you're the right person to give a girl her first experience.

TOLEN: She's an independent human being. Why should you say what's good for her? How old are you, Nancy?

NANCY: Seventeen.

TOLEN: There you are. (*Pause*.) Anyway, she's not really my type. I've had sufficient for today. I'm merely amusing myself. It's more subtle.

TOM: You know what happens to young girls alone in London, don't you?

NANCY: Yes—no—I——

TOM: You'd better find a Catholic Girls' Refuge.

NANCY: I'm not a Catholic.

TOM: You'll find the address in any ladies lavatory in any railway station.

NANCY: Oh—I——

TOLEN: How do you know?

NANCY: I think I ought to go—I——

(*Enter* COLIN *with tea things including milk in a bottle.*)

COLIN: That damned stuff in the passage. You'll have to move it.

TOM: I'm not having it in here.

COLIN: I'm not having it in the passage.

TOM: I'm not having it in here.

COLIN: When you take a furnished room, you take the furniture as well.

TOM: Not that furniture.

COLIN: What's wrong with the furniture?

TOM: I'm not having it in here. Put it on the bed. Take it to Copp Street.

COLIN: It's my furniture, you're not selling my furniture.

TOM: You're selling your bed.

COLIN: You're not selling my furniture.

TOM: We'll put it on the top landing.

TOLEN: Outside my room? I think not.

TOM: Inside your room.

COLIN: Oh. Let's have some tea.

(*They start pouring out tea.*)

TOLEN: What's the most frightening building in London?

COLIN: Great Ormond Street Hospital for Children.

(*Pause.*)

TOM: What's that?

COLIN: Great Ormond Street Hospital for Children.

NANCY: That's nice. It's true. That's a nice thing to say.

COLIN: Oh? Do you think so?

(TOLEN *touches* NANCY.)

TOM: Do you know how the elephant got the shape it

47

is? Well, there was once a little piggy animal, see? With two great big front teeth that stuck out. However, there are certain advantages in being big—you know, you can eat off trees and things—like horses——

TOLEN: For you this is remarkably incoherent.

TOM: Thanks. So this animal got big and it grew an enormous great long jaw so it could scoop up the vegetation. An enormous jaw, seven foot long—imagine! As big as a door! Now. A seven-foot jaw involves certain difficulties in getting the food from the front of your jaw to the back . . .

TOLEN: Biscuits?

TOM: It had to use its upper lip to shovel the garbage along.

COLIN: Aren't there some chocolate?

TOM: I ate them. Well, the creature's upper lip began to grow. It grew so big it began to do all the work and the creature didn't bother to use its seven-foot jaw. Now, as you know, any organ not in constant use atrophies so the jaw began to shrivel. (*To* TOLEN) Not that you need . . .

NANCY: Tea?

TOM: *But* the two front teeth——

NANCY: More tea?

TOM: Remained. So you are left with an animal having an extraordinarily long upper jaw and two big front teeth. You're left with an elephant. No problem at all. Yes I would, please.

(TOLEN *touches* NANCY'*s arm*.)

NANCY: D'you like it? It's new.

48

TOLEN: You should paint that wall straight away or it'll patch up.

TOM: What?

TOLEN: It will dry blotchy.

TOM: Yes. That's a good idea. Yes!

TOLEN: You wanted to see me?

COLIN: Eh?

TOLEN: That's right.

COLIN: Wanted to see you?

TOLEN: You will.

COLIN: What d'you——

TOLEN: Watch this.

COLIN: What do you mean?

TOM: In cold blood, Colin. In cold blood.

TOLEN: I'll show you how.

TOM: Nancy! (*Angry.*) You should go when you're told.

(TOLEN *takes a copy of* Honey *and lies on the bed.*)

NANCY: Would you like something behind your head?

TOLEN: There is a pillow in the passage.

(NANCY *exits, returns with pillow.*)

TOLEN: Why don't you look at me?

NANCY: I can't.

TOLEN: Why can't you?

NANCY: I'll—I'll——

TOLEN: What?

NANCY: I'll laugh.

TOLEN: Why?

NANCY: You'll make me laugh.

TOLEN: Why?

NANCY: You will.

TOLEN: Will I?

NANCY: Yes.

TOLEN : Will I?

NANCY : Yes.

TOLEN : Look at me, laugh! Go on! Look at me, laugh, look at me, go on, look at me, laugh, look at me, look at me.

(*She laughs. She stops laughing. He might kiss her.*)

NANCY : No, no.

COLIN : Ha!

TOLEN : You idiot. Fool.

(*Pause.*)

TOM : Do you like my room?

NANCY : What?

TOM : My room.

NANCY : What! It's not much. There's not much to sit on.

TOM : Sit on the piano.

NANCY : (*irritated*). Aw!

TOM : They clutter up the place so I really must get them on the wall.

NANCY : What?

TOM : The chairs. On the wall.

NANCY : What? Oh, it doesn't matter.

TOM : To get them off the floor. Have I said anything to upset you, Tolen?

TOLEN : Nothing you said could possibly upset me. (*Pause.*) Why do you try and find rational reasons for your childish impulses?

TOM : Do I disturb you?

TOLEN : You make me smile.

TOM : Ooh! He's annoyed. Oh yes, he's annoyed. Be careful or you might lose control. Ah well. Back to work. Pass me another cup of tea, Nancy.

NANCY : What?

50

TOM : Get me another cup of tea, there's a dear.

NANCY : What do you think I am?

TOM : Oh. (*Pause.*) Sorry.

NANCY : Oh all right. (*She pours out tea for* TOM.)

TOM : Thanks.

NANCY : (*to* TOLEN). Do you want some?

TOLEN : No.

(NANCY *pours out tea for herself. Long pause.*)
All right. She's all yours.

COLIN : Eh?

TOLEN : You have a try.

COLIN : What? Me?

TOLEN : Yes.

(*Long pause.*)

COLIN : Has Cardiff got big docks?

NANCY : What?

COLIN : Has Cardiff got big d-docks?

NANCY : Why ask me?

COLIN : Welsh. I mean—aren't you—don't you come
from Wales?

NANCY : No.

COLIN : It was the name—Jones.

NANCY : Where d'you say the Y.W. was?

COLIN : Oh, it's in Martin's Grove. You have to take a
27 bus, get off at the top of Church Street and
walk down on the left until——

NANCY : It far?

COLIN : Pardon?

NANCY : Is it far?

COLIN : No, not very.

NANCY : Good. I'm going.

COLIN : What?

NANCY : I'm off. I said I'm going. And as for you. As for
you Mr. Mr. Mr. only one name. Mr. no name.

51

As for you. As for you. As for you . . .
(TOLEN *laughs.*)
That's my *Honey*. Give me my *Honey*.
COLIN : I'll take you. I said I'll take you there.
TOLEN : You want your magazine?
(*She retreats.* TOLEN *follows her. She cannot retreat farther. She slaps him. He kisses her.*)
See? It's not difficult.
(NANCY *bursts into tears.*)
TOM : Well that's that. I need this room, Tolen.
TOLEN : Expecting someone?
TOM : Maybe.
TOLEN : Man or woman? (*Pause.*) Are you a homosexual?
TOM : No. Thanks all the same.
(*Exit* TOLEN.)
COLIN : Why do you like annoying him?
TOM : He was annoyed, wasn't he? He's softening up. Ha ha! Now he'll play gramophone records and make telephone calls. Really Colin, what a mess, suppose the Queen were to come. Oh this wall, this sickening, everlasting wall, it's enormous, it goes on for ever. I'm fed up with it. Here.
(*Gives* COLIN *a brush.*)
COLIN : Eh? What's this for?
(TOM *gives* NANCY *a brush.*)
TOM : Only the end bit, the plain bit, the uncreative bit, the bit that don't need genius.
COLIN : You want us to paint the wall?
TOM : The white bit, the boring bit. I'm sick of it.
COLIN : You're so damned lazy.
TOM : Attack it. Attack it.
COLIN : And messy.

52

NANCY: Yes! Yes! you yes! (*She attacks wall.*) You ha ha! Yes (*mumbling between her teeth*). Yes! Um hm um hm!

TOM: A dear girl. A darling girl. There. That's right. (*Exit* TOM.)

COLIN: Here?

TOM: (*off*). Here?

COLIN: The end.

TOM: (*off*). The window end?

COLIN: Yes.

TOM: (*entering*). That's right.
(*Enter* TOM *with a sheet which he ties round* NANCY. *She takes her jacket off and gives it to him.*)

TOM: Ah yes, that's nice. Faster, serfs! (*Pause.*) Elephants. (*Pause.*) The Indians keep elephants like we keep cows.—I was wondering how big an elephant's udder was. My God, imagine it swishing around. Do you know, in Walt Disney's early films there were cows and the censor cut the udders out so he put brassieres on them, imagine! . . . Jersey cows wear brassieres, it's true. Jersey cows wear brassieres. Something wrong here, cows shouldn't need brassieres. Human beings need them because they stand upright. They used to go on all fours, so they hung downwards—vertically—now they stand upright and it puts on this terrible strain . . .
(NANCY *is laughing.*)
All right, all right. It's true.

COLIN: Oh——

TOM: Eh?

COLIN: I wish you wouldn't show off.

53

TOM: (*to* NANCY). Hi! (*To* COLIN) I don't show off.

COLIN· You do.

TOM: (*restraining* NANCY). Colin wishes I wouldn't show off.

COLIN: Well you do show off.

TOM: I don't.

COLIN: You do. Stop slapping it.

NANCY: I like slapping.

COLIN: It's splashing.

NANCY: So what?

COLIN: It's dripping.

NANCY: I don't care. I don't care.

COLIN: Don't get so excited.

NANCY: You're talking. I hear you.

COLIN: Look at her. Look at her.

TOM: I see her.

NANCY: So what.

TOM: (*shepherding* NANCY *to a bit of wall away from his careful painting*). Watch it—yes—there's a— and now—that's right—more left.

NANCY: What's the difference between an elephant and a pillar box?

COLIN: They can neither of them ride a bicycle.

NANCY: You knew!

COLIN: What? What?

NANCY: I can reach higher than you.

COLIN: (*holding up his arm*). Heard it before.

NANCY: Yes, I can.

TOM: I don't show off.

COLIN: What? No, you can't.

NANCY: I can.

COLIN: You can't.

TOM: I do——

NANCY: I can——

54

TOM: —sometimes——

NANCY: —look——

COLIN: You don't—I mean——

NANCY: I can reach higher than you——

COLIN: Ouch!

NANCY: What?

COLIN: It's all run up my elbow. Oh.

TOM: You're dripping everywhere. There's a cloth in the kitchen.

(*Exit* COLIN. *Telephone rings* (*off*). *Pause. Enter* TOLEN.)

TOLEN: It's for you.

TOM: Man or woman?

TOLEN: Woman.

(*Exit* TOM. *Pause.* TOLEN *moves to help* NANCY *off with sheet. She avoids him.*)

TOLEN: No one's going to rape you.

NANCY: Oh!

TOLEN: (*laughing*). Girls never get raped unless they want it.

NANCY: Oh!

TOLEN: I'm sorry about—what happened.

NANCY: That's——

TOLEN: It was clumsy—very——

NANCY: That's all right.

TOLEN: It was because they were here—the clumsiness I mean——

NANCY: Was it?

TOLEN: In a way, in a way.

NANCY: Oh.

TOLEN: Don't you believe me?

NANCY: I don't know—I——

TOLEN: Please——

NANCY: I——

TOLEN : Please believe me.

NANCY : It doesn't matter.

TOLEN : It does matter, it matters very much. (*Pause.*) It matters very much to me. (*Pause.*) How sweet you are. Such a sweet face, such sweetness. (*Pause. He kisses her.*) Ssh . . . ssh . . . Come . . . come up . . . come upstairs . . .

NANCY : Oh . . . oh . . .

TOLEN : Come up to my room . . .

NANCY : Oh . . . oh . . . no . . .

TOLEN : You like music? I've got some records upstairs . . . I'll play you some records.
(*Enter* COLIN.)

COLIN : Well, let's get on—oh— . . . Where are you going? Are you going out? To find the Y.W.? I'll come too.

TOLEN : What?

COLIN : I'll come as well.

TOLEN : Where?

COLIN : To find it.

TOLEN : What?

COLIN : The Y.W.
(*Pause.*)

TOLEN : Why don't you go?

COLIN : Eh?

TOLEN : Why don't you go look for the Y.W.?

COLIN : Well, you're coming aren't you?
(TOLEN *is exasperated.*)
Well—you——

NANCY : Oh——

COLIN : Oh come on——

NANCY : I don't think I——

COLIN : Oh please——

NANCY : What about the cases?

COLIN: The cases?

NANCY: I can't go without them.

COLIN: He'll look after them.

NANCY: Who will?

COLIN: He will.

TOLEN: Me?

NANCY: Where are you going?

TOLEN: I'm going out.

NANCY: I'd like a walk.

COLIN: So would I.

NANCY: What about the cases?

COLIN: You stay here.

TOLEN: Why should I?

COLIN: You could stay here.

TOLEN: Why should I?

COLIN: You could look after the cases.

TOLEN: He can.

COLIN: Who can?

TOLEN: Tom can.

COLIN: He's upstairs. Can't they stay here?

NANCY: I need them at the Y.W.

(TOLEN *moves away*. NANCY *follows*.)

COLIN: Let's go look for the Y.W.

NANCY: Are you coming?

TOLEN: To the Y.W.?

COLIN: Well, let's you and me go.

NANCY: Well——

COLIN: Well——

NANCY: I don't think I really——

COLIN: You said you did.

NANCY: Did I?

COLIN: Yes.

NANCY: What about the cases?

TOLEN: Why don't you carry them?

COLIN: Me?

TOLEN: If you're going to the Y.W., why don't you carry them?

COLIN: Let's go for a walk.

NANCY: What about the cases?

TOLEN: You carry them.

COLIN: She!

TOLEN: Yes.

COLIN: She can't carry them.

TOLEN: She's already carried them. She carried them here.

COLIN: She can't carry them.

TOLEN: You carry them.

COLIN: I want both hands free.

(*Pause. Enter* TOM. TOLEN *starts to exit.*)

NANCY: Where you going?

TOLEN: Oh, anywhere. D'you want to?

NANCY: D'you want me to?

TOLEN: If you want to.

COLIN: Are you going to the Y.W.?

TOLEN: Maybe.

COLIN: I'll come too.

TOLEN: What about the cases?

(COLIN *picks up the cases.*)

COLIN: I'll come too.

(TOLEN *and* NANCY *exit.*)

TOM: Stay with them, Colin.

COLIN: Eh?

TOM: Stick with them.

(*Exit* COLIN. TOLEN *and* NANCY *are seen to pass window, followed soon after by* COLIN. *Exit* TOM. *Heavy dragging and banging off. Enter* TOM *looking very pleased with himself, takes bed to bits and drags it off. More banging. Enter* TOM *exhausted. Drinks milk. Exits with tray. Re-enters and resumes painting.* TOLEN *and* NANCY *pass window. Door is tried (off).* TOLEN *and* NANCY *enter through window. Both are laughing a good deal.*)

TOLEN: That door blocked again?

TOM: Been moving a few things.

TOLEN: And if you push it under—ooops! (NANCY *laughs*) and over—ooops! (NANCY *laughs*.)
(*Enter* COLIN *through window.*

TOM: You look very seasick.

COLIN: Shut up.
(COLIN *thrusts carrier bag on his head.* NANCY *is pretty hysterical.* TOLEN *works her up, kissing and laughing.* TOM *intensifies the atmosphere by beating a rhythm on bed or step-ladder, possibly using mouth music as well.*)

TOLEN: We'll go and listen to those gramophone records.
(*Exit* TOLEN *and* NANCY. TOM *stops beating. Pause. Large crash (off). Enter* TOLEN.)

TOLEN: Who put that stuff on the stairs?

TOM: Oh, are the stairs blocked?

TOLEN: I can't get up to my room.

TOM: Oh, can't you?
(*Enter* NANCY.)

NANCY: Why's the wardrobe on the stairs—and the bed—the stairs are blocked . . .
(TOLEN *grabs her.*)
Oh! You're hurting me!

TOM: Stop. Stop that.

NANCY: Let me go! Let me go! Let me go!
(*She escapes but not before* TOLEN *has hurt and thoroughly frightened her.*)

Don't touch me! (TOM *and* COLIN *attempt to comfort her but they only excite her more.*) Keep off! Keep off! D'you hear? Keep away! Don't touch me! You—you—you—don't touch me! You don't touch me. All right? All right? . . . Now, now then, now . . . what's—what's up? What is it, eh? Yes? What you—what you want with me?—what you want—What you trying on, eh? What you trying to do? What is it, eh? What you want—you—you—you . . . . . . Smartie! Smartie! Mr. You—Smart! Mr. Smartie! You think you're—you're. You think you're all right, you think you're pretty clever. You think—you—you think you're all right . . . . . . You do, don't you, Mr. Smartie—tight— tight trousers! Mr. Tight Trousers! Mr. Narrow Trousers! You think you're the cat's—you think you're . . . I'll show you . . . I'll show you, Mr. Tight Trousers. Just you don't come near me, d'you hear? Just you don't come near me—come near me, d'you hear? Come near me! I'll show you, Mr. Tight Trousers! Tight Trousers! Yes! Yes! Come near me! Come near me! Come near me! Come! Come! Come! Come! Come!
(TOLEN *laughs and walks away.* NANCY *moans and collapses.* COLIN *somehow catches her as she falls.*)

COLIN: She's fainted!

TOM: Lucky there was someone to catch her.

(*End of Act Two*)

ACT THREE

Before the curtain rises there is a loud banging and crashing, mixed with shouts and cries.
Curtain up.
COLIN *is holding* NANCY *like a sack of potatoes.* TOM *and* TOLEN *are just finishing putting up the bed.*

TOM: Give it a bash! And so—oops! A bedmaker, that's you Tolen, a master bed-wright. O.K. Has she come round yet?
COLIN: Come round?
TOM: Is she still out?
COLIN: Out?
TOM: Oh, he's a thick one. This way.
COLIN: I'm not thick, she's heavy.
TOM: Don't drop her. Now we've got this out of the passage, Tolen, you can go upstairs to bed. We'll put her here to rest. Sling her over. . . . Not like that!
COLIN: You said sling.
TOM: She's in a faint, fainted, can't defend herself.
(*They get* NANCY *on the bed.*)
NANCY: Oh . . . oh dear . . . oh dear . . . I do feel . . . I think I'm going to be——
TOM: Sick?
(NANCY *nods.*)
Not here.

(COLIN *holds out bucket.* TOM *dashes to door and opens it.*)

Bathroom.

(*Exit* NANCY *followed by* TOM. *Pause.* TOLEN *goes to door. Opens it and listens a moment, then closes door and bolts it.*)

COLIN: What are you doing?

TOLEN: I don't want to be interrupted, Colin. I don't want Tom to interrupt me. I have something I wish to discuss with you, Colin.

COLIN: Oh, I see. . . . But this is Tom's room.

TOLEN: This is your room, Colin, your room. You are the landlord, Colin. The house belongs to you so this is your room, not Tom's. It's for you to say whose room this is, Colin. Who lives here.

COLIN: Oh, yes—er——

TOLEN: There is something I would like to discuss with you, Colin. An idea I had.

COLIN: Oh?

TOLEN: Are you listening carefully, Colin? This is very important to you.

COLIN: Oh?

TOLEN: You know that you need help, Colin. You do know that, don't you?

COLIN: Mm.

TOLEN: Now tell me, Colin, how many women have you had?

COLIN: Mm . . .

TOLEN: Two women. Only two. And you were late starting weren't you, Colin? Very late. Not until last year. And Carol left you how many months ago?

COLIN: Mm . . .

TOLEN: Six months ago. That's right, isn't it. Two

women in two years. Some of us have more
women in two days. Now I can help you, you
know that, don't you?

COLIN: Mm.

TOLEN: I have a suggestion to make to you, Colin. A
suggestion which you will find very interesting
and which will help you very much. (*Pause.*)
Now as you know, Colin, I have a number of
friends. *Men*. And they can help you Colin, as I
can help you. I am thinking particularly of Rory
McBride. Rory McBride.

COLIN: Oh.

TOLEN: Rory McBride is a man, Colin, a clever man,
a gifted man, a man I can respect. He knows a
great many things, Colin. Rory McBride was
doing things at thirteen that you haven't ever
done, Colin; things that you don't even know
about.

COLIN: What sort of things?

TOLEN: In a moment, Colin. First I will tell you my
suggestion. Now, as you know, I have a number
of regular girl friends. You know that, don't
you?

COLIN: Mm.

TOLEN: Regular women, Colin. Women I regularly
make. And Rory McBride has a number of
regular women too. Perhaps not quite as many
as I have, Colin, but several. Now. Quite
recently, Rory and I were talking—comparing
notes—and we decided it would be a good idea
if we saw each other more often . . . if even we
were to live near each other.

COLIN: Oh?

TOLEN: Yes, Colin . . . perhaps in the same house . . . and that we would share our women.

COLIN: Oh?

TOLEN: Share our women.

COLIN: Oh!

TOLEN: Of course Rory realizes that it may, in a sense, be dangerous for him. He may lose a few of his women. However, Rory is well aware that, in the long run, he will profit by the arrangement; he will learn much, Colin, from the women who have been with me.

COLIN: (*agreeing*). Mm.

TOLEN: Now this is the suggestion I have to make. I would consider allowing you to come in on this arrangement.

COLIN: Oh!

TOLEN: Yes, Colin. You have so much to learn and I would like to help you. I feel you deserve to be helped. I would allow you to come in with Rory and me, share our women. I think you would learn a great deal, Colin.

COLIN: Oh yes.

TOLEN: It would be a privilege for you, a great privilege.

COLIN: Oh, yes, I see that.

TOLEN: I was sure you would appreciate it. I'm sure Rory will agree to this, Colin. I will ask him.

COLIN: Do you think he will?

TOLEN: If I ask him, Colin, he will agree. (*Pause.*) Now what I suggest, Colin, is that Rory moves into this house.

COLIN: Mm?

TOLEN: In here.

COLIN: Oh . . .

TOLEN: What's the matter, Colin?

64

COLIN : But there's no room. There's you and me
and——

TOLEN : There is this room, Colin. The room you let to
Tom. (*Pause.*) Remember this is your room.
You are the landlord. Rory could have this
room and . . .

(TOM *yells* (*off*) *and bangs door.*)

Rory McBride has a Chinese girl, Colin, slinky,
very nice, do very well for you.

COLIN : Chinese?

TOLEN : It's only a question of experience. Of course
you'll never be quite so——

COLIN : Good as——

TOLEN : Me, but——

COLIN : But still——

TOLEN : Oh yes, I don't doubt——

COLIN : You really think——

TOLEN : Certainly!

COLIN : Chinese!

(*Enter* TOM *through window.*)

TOM : What the hell d'you think you're doing? Why
d'you bloody lock the door, Tolen? You bloody
remember this is my room.

(*He unbolts door.*)

TOLEN : Oh no, Tom, this is Colin's room.

TOM : Eh? What's going on here?

(*Small crash upstairs.*)

(*Yelling.*) Stop that. What the hell's she up to
now? Where's her bag? She wants her bleeding
bag. I tell you she's gone bloody funny like a
bleeding windmill.

(*Cry off.* TOLEN *crosses the room.*)

TOLEN : Can you not control your women, Tom?

(*Exit* TOM. TOLEN *crosses the room again.*)

TOLEN: And a German girl.

COLIN: German!

(COLIN *crosses the room imitating* TOLEN.)

TOLEN: Hold your head up, Colin. Head up! Don't stick your chin out. Keep your belly in. Bend your arms slightly at the elbows—not quite so—that's better. They should swing freely from your shoulders. . . . Not both together! Keep your head up! Move! Move! Move! Move! Feel it coming from your shoulders Colin, from your chest! From your gut! From your loin! More loin! More gut, man! Loin! Loin! Move! Move! Move! Move! Keep your head up! Authority, Colin! Feel it rippling through you! Authority! Keep your head up! Authority! Authority!

COLIN: Authority.

TOLEN: Authority! Move! Move! Move! Move! Authority!

TOM: (*off*). You can have a cup of tea and . . .

NANCY: (*off*). Tea!

TOM: (*off*). Tea.

NANCY: (*off*). I won't touch it.

(*Enter* NANCY *wrapped in a blanket*.)

TOM: (*entering*). For God's sake make her some tea.

NANCY: I won't touch it. What's that?

TOM: What's what?

NANCY: That.

TOM: We've lugged this thing in here so you can lie down. Now lie down.

NANCY: I never asked you to bring it in.

TOM: You——

NANCY: Don't swear.

(COLIN *walks about the stage*.)

You're not getting me on that thing again I tell

66

you. Putting that thing together again to tempt
a girl. Hiding it up passages. Stuffing it here and
there. What d'you think I am? Eh? Eh? Don't
you hear? Can't you hear what I say?
(NANCY *bares her teeth and growls at* COLIN. *He
is momentarily disconcerted then ignores her and
struts up and down again.*)
An open invitation if you ask me. Ask me! Go
on ask me! Well somebody ask me . . . please
. . . (*Pause.*) A nasty situation. Dear me, yes.
Very nasty, a particularly vicious sense of—
criminal, yes, that's it—positively criminal. They
ought to be told, somebody should—I shall
phone them, phone them—the police, Scotland
Yard, Whitehall one two one two (*she catches
sight of* COLIN *walking up and down*) one two
one two (*she repeats one two one two as often as
necessary*).
(COLIN *picks up the rhythm and they begin to
work each other up.* NANCY *starts to bang the
rhythm.* COLIN *stamps about and slaps himself
until eventually he hurts himself.* NANCY *is
temporarily assuaged.*)
TOM : That's an interesting movement you've got
there, Colin.
COLIN : Oh, d'you think so?
TOM : Very interesting.
COLIN : Tolen taught it me.
TOM : Oh yes?
COLIN : It's got authority.
TOM : Come again?
COLIN : Authority.
TOM : Ah. Let's see it again . . . ah.
(COLIN *demonstrates, then* TOM *has a go.*)

COLIN : You've got to walk from your gut.

TOM : Eh?

COLIN : Your gut.

TOM : Oh I see. I see, I see. Bucket!

COLIN : Eh?

TOM : For a helmet. Bucket! Bucket! Jump to it!
Don't keep me waiting. Bucket!

COLIN : Oh.

(COLIN *jumps for the bucket, offers it to* TOM *who
puts it on* COLIN's *head.*)

TOM : Now I'll show you what authority's really,
Colin. Much more impressive than a carrier—a
helmet. Dominating, brutal.

(TOM *starts banging a 4/4 rhythm and singing the
"Horst Wessel".*)

Ra ra ra ra, ra ra ra ra, march! March! March!
March! Get on with it! Ra ra ra ra.

(NANCY *picks up the 4/4 rhythm and the tune.*)

March! Damn you! March! Jams, guns, guts,
butter! Jams, guns, guts, butter! Boots! Boots!
Boots! Boots! Boots for crushing! Boots for
smashing! Sieg heil! Sieg heil! Ha!

(COLIN *gets rid of the bucket.*)

What's the matter? What's up? Don't you like
it? I thought you loved it. Tolen loves it, don't
you, Tolen? Tolen loves it.

COLIN : Tolen doesn't do that.

TOM : Not so loud maybe, but the same general idea. I
think it's funnier louder, don't you, Tolen?

COLIN : Shut up.

TOM : Just look at Tolen's boots.

(*Pause.* NANCY *jumps up and down.*)

NANCY : Grrr.

TOM : (*disregarding* NANCY *and speaking to* TOLEN).

When I die I could be reincarnated as a sea
anemone. It doesn't affect my attitude to death
one little bit but it does affect my attitude to
sea anemones.

A sea anemone with a crew cut would starve to
death. (*Pause.*) Your ears are going red. They're
pulsating red and blue. No, I'm exaggerating.
One is anyway. The one nearest me. (*Pause.*)
That white horse you see in the park could be a
zebra synchronized with the railings.

(TOLEN *moves away.* TOM *looks very pleased.*)

NANCY : I wouldn't touch it if you made it.

TOM : Eh?

NANCY : I wouldn't.

TOM : Made what?

NANCY : Tea.

TOM : (*to* COLIN). You'd better make some.

COLIN : (*disgruntled*). Oh.

TOM : Shall I tell you a story?

(*Exit* COLIN.)

I know you'd like to hear about the kangaroo—
the kangaroo. You heard me. Did you? Now of
course you know that the baby kangaroo lives
in its mother's pouch. Don't you. Go on,
commit yourself.

NANCY : Oh, all right.

TOM : Don't be so cautious. This one is true and pure.
All my stories are true unless I say so. Well, the
baby kangaroo is born about two inches long
and as soon as it's born it climbs into its
mother's pouch—how does it climb? Never
mind, it fights its way through the fur . . .

(COLIN *enters balefully and sets down a tray and
exits.*)

When it gets inside the pouch the baby kangaroo finds one large, solid nipple. Just one. The baby latches on to this nipple and then it, the nipple, swells and swells and swells until it's shaped something like a door knob in the baby's mouth. And there the baby kangaroo stays for four months, four solid months. What an almighty suck! Isn't that interesting? Doesn't it interest you as a facet of animal behaviour so affecting human behaviour? Doesn't it make you marvel at the vast family of which God made us part? Oh well . . .

(*Pause.*)

NANCY: What happened?

TOM: What happened when?

NANCY: You know when.

TOM: No, I do not.

NANCY: You know when.

(*Enter* COLIN *with teapot.* COLIN *pours out tea in silence. Hands a cup to* TOLEN, *goes with a cup to* NANCY.)

What's that?

COLIN: Eh?

TOM: Tea.

NANCY: I'm not having any. I'm not touching it. He's put something in it.

COLIN: Eh?

TOM: Put something in it?

NANCY: Oh yes, he's put something in it.

TOM: Don't be so daft.

NANCY: I'm not touching it.

TOM: But——

NANCY: I'm not.

TOM: What should he put in it? There's absolutely

nothing in it. Nothing at all—look—ugh!—
Sugar!
(*Pause.*)

NANCY : I like sugar.

COLIN : Two.

NANCY : What?

COLIN : Two lumps.

NANCY : I take two.

COLIN : I know.
(*Pause.* NANCY *takes the tea and drinks. Long pause.*)

NANCY : I've been raped. (*Pause.*) I have.

TOLEN : I beg your pardon.

NANCY : You heard.

COLIN : I didn't.

NANCY : I've been raped.
(TOLEN *sneers audibly.*)

COLIN : What!

NANCY : I have been—it was just after—when I fainted—
there by the—before I went up with—when I
fainted. I was raped.
(TOLEN *sneers.*)

COLIN : When she says——

NANCY : I have been, you did——

COLIN : Does she mean really—I mean, actually?

TOM : What else?

NANCY : Rape. Rape. I—I've been——

COLIN : But——

NANCY : Raped.

COLIN : But you haven't.

NANCY : I have.

COLIN : No one has——

NANCY : Rape.

COLIN : But we've been here all the time, all of us.

71

NANCY: Huh!

COLIN: You know we have.

TOLEN: A vivid imagination, that's what's the matter with her.

NANCY: Eh?

COLIN: Oh?

TOM: Watch it.

TOLEN: Take no notice of her.

NANCY: Eh?

TOLEN: Ignore her.

NANCY: What? Rape?

TOM: You be careful, Tolen.

NANCY: Rape! I been——

TOLEN: She quite simply wishes to draw attention to herself.

NANCY: (*a little unsure*). Oh?

TOLEN: She has fabricated a fantasy that we have raped her. First because she wants us to take notice of her and second because she really would like to be raped.

NANCY: Eh?

COLIN: Would you mind saying that again?

TOLEN: Her saying that we have raped her is a fantasy. She has fabricated this fantasy because she really does want to be raped; she wants to be the centre of attention. The two aims are, in a sense, identical. The fabrication that we have raped her satisfactorily serves both purposes.

COLIN: Oh.

NANCY: What's that word mean? Fabricated?

TOLEN: Made it up.

NANCY: (*a bit nonplussed*). Oh no. Oh no. Not that. I know, oh yes. I'm not having that sort of—I know, oh yes. I'm the one that knows. You've

had your fun and—and—there! It was there!
You've had your fun and now I feel funny,
queer, sick. I know, you're not coping with a—
I'm not a fool you know—I'm not a ninny. . . .
No, no, I didn't make it up . . . fabricated . . .
fabricated . . . fabricated . . .

TOM : (*to* TOLEN). What'll you do if she tells everyone
you raped her?

TOLEN : What?

TOM : There's a methodist minister lives two doors
down. Suppose she was to yell out of the
window? By God you'd look silly, you'd look
right foolish. I'd give a lot to see that.

TOLEN : Are you mad?

TOM : (*to* NANCY). Don't let him off so easily love.

NANCY : Eh?

TOM : (*to* TOLEN). What'll you do if she yells down the
street?

NANCY : Rape! They done me! Rape! You done me! You
did! Rape! Rape! Rape! Rape! Rape! (*At
window*) Rape! (*etc. as necessary*).

TOLEN : Shut the window.
(TOLEN *goes for* NANCY.)

NANCY : Rape!
(TOLEN *gets her neatly under control and keeps his
hand over her mouth.*)

TOM : Try and keep your dignity on that one.

COLIN : Mind she doesn't bite.

TOLEN : Shut the window.
(COLIN *shuts the window.* TOLEN *releases* NANCY.)

NANCY : You don't want me yelling down the street, do
you?

TOLEN : We don't want the trivial inconvenience.

73

NANCY: You're scared they'll hear and lock you up.

TOLEN: I do not intend to expose myself to trivial indignities from petty officials.

NANCY: You're worried. You're scared. You're afraid. I'll tell. I will tell!

COLIN: Eh?

NANCY: The police. The Y.W. I'll report you. That's it. The lot. Them all. I'll tell them how you raped me—how you—I'll tell them. The coppers. The Y.W.

TOM: Whew!

NANCY: All the lurid details! All the horrid facts! *News of the World*. TV. Read all about it! Rape! Rape! Just you wait! You'll get ten years for this!

TOM: She means it.

TOLEN: She's simply drawing attention to herself.

COLIN: Means what?

TOM: She means to tell everyone we raped her. Right. (*Putting* TOLEN *on the spot*.) In that case he must rape her.

COLIN: Eh?

TOLEN: I beg your pardon?

TOM: In that case she must be raped by him.

NANCY: I'm not having it twice.

TOM: You want her to keep quiet.

TOLEN: I do not propose to allow her to expose . . .

TOM: (*cutting him short*). Right. You say she's made this up because she really does want to be raped.

COLIN: Well?

TOM: If he wants to keep her quiet he must rape her. According to what he says—and he's probably right—that's the only thing will satisfy her.

74

COLIN : If she's raped she'll be the centre of attention, that's it!

TOM : Just so. What do you say?

(*The men are talking about* NANCY *but, in a sense, have forgotten her. She is resentful.*)

NANCY : Rape!

TOM : What do you say, Tolen?

(*Pause.*)

TOLEN : It's your idea. Why don't you rape her?

TOM : I like her yelling down the street.

(*Pause.*)

TOLEN : Colin?

COLIN : What me? Oh no. I couldn't.

(*Pause.*)

NANCY : Rape!

TOLEN : I never yet came to a woman under duress and certainly never because I was forced to it. Because she demanded it. Because I had to buy her silence. I shall not now.

(NANCY *explodes round the room.*)

NANCY : Ray! Ray! Ray! Ray! Ray! (*continue as long as necessary*).

COLIN : Stop her!

TOLEN : Don't let her——

TOM : Whoops! Whoops!

TOLEN : Near the——

COLIN : What eh?

TOLEN : Shut the door!

COLIN : Ow!

TOLEN : ——door!

TOM : Door? Door?

COLIN : Door?

(*A chase. Finally* NANCY *exits down left by mistake.* COLIN *slams door and bolts it.*)

75

TOLEN : The front. The front door. She'll get out the front. Colin!

(*Exit* COLIN *through window. Banging (off) at front door. Re-enter* COLIN.)

COLIN : No, she won't. It's blocked.

(*Pause.*)

TOM : She smashed up the bathroom. She might——

(*Pause.*)

TOLEN : My records!

(TOLEN *throws himself on the door. Enter* NANCY *barefoot. She wears her pleated skirt thus: her right arm through the placket, the waist band running over her right shoulder and under her left arm. She carries her underclothes, which she scatters gaily.*)

NANCY : Shove you in jug! Put you in jail! One for the road! Long for a stretch! Just you wait! I'll tell!

(*Pause.*)

TOM : That's not how a skirt is usually worn, still it's bigger than a bathing costume.

COLIN : It's not a bathing costume.

NANCY : I shall sue you for paternity.

TOM : Now listen, Nancy.

NANCY : All of you.

TOM : Nancy.

NANCY : Don't Nancy me.

TOM : (NANCY *ad libs through speech*). Look love— don't say anything for a minute. Now look, we haven't raped you—but—just a moment—Now listen, everything's happening so fast you must give us a chance to think. I mean you're a reasonable girl, Nancy, an intelligent girl, give us a chance now, just give us a chance like a reasonable, rational, intelligent girl, just let us

76

talk for one moment. No yelling and no dashing off anywhere.

NANCY: It's a trap.

TOM: No it isn't. I promise. It's pax for one minute.

NANCY: All right. I'll give you one minute.

TOM: That's not enough.

NANCY: Two minutes.

TOM: Five.

NANCY: Three.

TOM: Done.

NANCY: Three minutes and no more. Then I'll start yelling again. Lend me a wrist watch.

TOM: Oh very well. Colin!

NANCY: And if you're naughty and cheat I can smash it.

COLIN: Oh I say——

TOM: Oh come on, Colin.

(COLIN *hands over his watch.* NANCY *climbs step-ladder.*)

Author's Note: the following scene falls into four sections.

1st section: Introduction to the scene: The three confer.)

TOM: Now, Tolen.

TOLEN: The situation is quite clear.

COLIN: Not to me it isn't.

TOM: You've got to rape her.

TOLEN: Please be quiet, Tom.

NANCY: (*while the others confer*).

I've been raped, I've been raped,

I've been raped, raped, raped,

I've been raped, I've been raped, I've been raped.

I've been raped, I've been raped,

77

I've been raped, raped, raped,
I've been raped, I've been raped, I've been raped.

TOM: Oh go on.

TOLEN: An impasse has been reached.

COLIN: She believes we've raped her.

TOM: She's convinced herself.

TOLEN: She's made it up to draw attention to herself and because she wants it.

TOM: She is prepared to report us.

COLIN: Yes, yes.

TOM: Tolen doesn't want that.

COLIN: No, no.

TOM: But he's not prepared to do the other thing.

COLIN: What are we going to do?

(*Pause.*)

TOLEN: She must be examined by a competent physician.

COLIN: What?

TOLEN: A doctor. If she's a virgin——

TOM: Not interfered with——

TOLEN: That lets us out!

COLIN: What if she's not?

(*Pause.*)

TOM: If she's not a virgin she could say we raped her and we'd have a job to prove otherwise.

TOLEN: She must be a virgin.

TOM: Why should she be?

TOLEN: Well, take a look at her.

NANCY: Two minutes gone. One minute to go.

TOLEN: Obviously a virgin.

TOM: I don't see why, it doesn't necessarily follow.

COLIN: Follow what?

NANCY: Finished?

TOM: No.

NANCY: Ninety seconds to go.

78

COLIN: Mind the watch.

NANCY: Rape!

TOLEN: Don't get so excited, Colin.

COLIN: It's my watch.

2nd section: TOM begins to enjoy the humour of the situation, and states his attitude; so that TOLEN also states *his* attitude.

TOM: Since you take this attitude, there seems no rational course other than to negotiate. Open negotiation.

TOLEN: Negotiate!

TOM: Negotiate.

TOLEN: Negotiate with a woman. Never.

TOM: Then what is your suggestion?

TOLEN: Authority.

COLIN: Oh?

TOLEN: Authority.

COLIN: Ah!

TOLEN: In all his dealings with women a man must act with promptness and authority—even, if need be, force.

COLIN: Force?

TOM: Force?

TOLEN: Force.

3rd section: COLIN decides that TOLEN's attitude is correct.

TOM: I cannot agree to force and certainly not to brutality.

TOLEN: Never negotiate.

TOM: Calm, calmth.

NANCY: Sixty seconds.

TOLEN: Force.

TOM: Negotiate. Parley, parley.
TOLEN: Negotiate with a woman——
TOM: Calm.
TOLEN: Never! Force!
COLIN: He's——
TOLEN: Force. Force.
COLIN: For——
TOM: Calm, calm, calmth.
TOLEN: Force, force. Never negotiate.
COLIN: For—for——
TOM: No brutality!
COLIN: Force!
TOLEN: Never negotiate! Eh?
COLIN: Force! Force!
TOM: Oh!
COLIN: Force! Force! In dealing with a w-w-w-w—
NANCY: Forty seconds to go!
COLIN: —w-woman a man must act with promptness and authority.
TOLEN: Force.
COLIN: Force.

4th section: COLIN is precipitated into a forceful course of action.

TOM: Parley, negotiate.
TOLEN: Authority.
TOM: Parley.
TOLEN: Force.
COLIN: Force.
TOM: No, no, parley, parley!
COLIN: Force.
TOLEN: Force.
NANCY: Twenty.
TOM: Parley, parley.

80

TOLEN: No, no. Force.

COLIN: For! For! For! He's right!

NANCY: Ten seconds to go.

COLIN: Force.

> (*The following should tumble across each other as the excitement mounts.*)

TOLEN: Force.

TOM: Parley.

NANCY: Eight.

COLIN: Force.

TOLEN: Never negotiate.

TOM: Calm.

COLIN: He's right, he's absolutely——

TOLEN: Force.

NANCY: Four.

COLIN: A man——

NANCY: Three.

COLIN: Must——

NANCY: Two.

COLIN: Use——

NANCY: One.

COLIN: Force. (*Slight pause.*) Shut up! Just you shut your—d'you hear! You're talking through you—Firmness! A firm hand! Spanking! See who's—I've been here all the time, d'you hear? All the time. You've not been raped. You have not. I know. So stop squawking. I know. I've been here all the time.

NANCY: Ah.

COLIN: I've been here all the time. So I can prove, prove, testify. I have seen nothing. You've not been raped. I know. I've been here all the time.

NANCY: Ah.

COLIN: Come on down now and get them on. Get your

clothes on. Come down, come down you silly little . . . little messer. You've not been raped, I know. I've been here all the time.

NANCY: You!

COLIN: I've been here all the time!

NANCY: You did it! It was you!

COLIN: I been here . . . eh?

NANCY: You! You! You! You! He's it! He did it! He raped me! He's been here all the time! He says so! He has! He did it! Yes, he raped me!

COLIN: Eh?

NANCY: You did it. You raped me. You did it. I'll report you.

COLIN: Me!

NANCY: You.

TOM: Him!

COLIN: Me!

NANCY: Yes, you. You been here all the time.

TOM: You, she says. She says you did it.

COLIN: Me.

NANCY: Yes, you did. You'll get ten years.

COLIN: Me, me? Me! Oh no. This is awful.

NANCY: You!

COLIN: You're making a terrible mistake.

NANCY: Oh no, not likely, I been here all the time.

COLIN: Oh, oh you are—tell her someone. Someone, Tolen, tell—her I didn't. No really, I mean——

NANCY: I got a head on my shoulders.

COLIN: I can see that but——

NANCY: That's it, you. You raped me.

COLIN: But—but I assure you—I mean——

NANCY: Not at all—it was you—it was him, oh yes.

COLIN: No, no, but really, I mean—me.

NANCY: That's him, officer, that's the one—him. Got

your handcuffs? Handcuffs. And the other one.
Right. This way, come sir, if you please——

COLIN: No! Tolen—Tom—please. I mean I didn't
really I didn't.

NANCY: Clothes!

COLIN: Clothes?

NANCY: Tore them off me.

COLIN: Tore the—oh no.

NANCY: Scattered.

COLIN: No.

NANCY: There they are.

TOM: Clear evidence.

NANCY: That face. You'd never know, they'd never
guess.

COLIN: Oh, wouldn't they?

NANCY: No girl would ever suspect.

COLIN: Oh?

NANCY: But underneath——

COLIN: What?

NANCY: Raving with lust.

COLIN: Oh no, I mean——

NANCY: Fangs dripping with blood.

COLIN: Oh.

NANCY: Bones of countless victims hidden in the
basement.

COLIN: We haven't got a basement. No! No! I mean I
didn't, really I didn't. I didn't rape you—I mean
I wouldn't—but well—this is terrible! Me! . . .
You really think I did?

NANCY: Of course.

COLIN: I mean you really do think I did?

NANCY: Yes.

COLIN: You really do!

NANCY: Wait till next Sunday. What's your job?

83

COLIN: Eh? Im a teacher.

NANCY: Schoolteacher rapes—rapes—rapes—Nancy Jones!

COLIN: Oh!

NANCY: Little did the pupils at—at——

COLIN: Tottenham Secondary Modern——

NANCY: Tottenham Secondary Modern realize that beneath the handsome exterior of their tall, fair-haired, blue-eyed schoolteacher there lurked the heart of a beast, lusting for the blood of innocent virgins—little did they—You wait till you see the *Sunday Pictorial*.

COLIN: Oh, I say, me. Me. Me. Oh I say. Oh. Oh. Do you really think——?

NANCY: What?

COLIN: I've got a handsome exterior?

NANCY: Well—rugged perhaps, rather than handsome. And strong.

COLIN: Oh.

NANCY: Oh yes, ever so. And lovely hands.

COLIN: Oh. Oh. Oh. . . . Are you—are you doing anything tonight?

NANCY: What?

COLIN: Are you doing anything tonight?

NANCY: Oh!

COLIN: Oh, please, I didn't mean that. I mean I didn't rape you, anyway, I mean, oh well. Look, I mean let's go to the pictures or something or a walk or a drink or anything please. I think you're simply—I mean—Oh golly—do you really think I did? I mean I didn't rape you but I would like to—I mean, I would like to take you to the pictures or something.

NANCY: Well, I don't know it doesn't seem quite—I mean after——

COLIN: Oh please——

NANCY: Well——

COLIN: The pictures or anything.

NANCY: Would you?

COLIN: Oh, yes, I would.

TOLEN: This I find all very amusing.

TOM: I thought you might.

TOLEN: Hilarious.

TOM: I've always admired your sense of humour.

COLIN: Eh?

TOM: Well done. Very good. You're getting on very nicely, Colin. Much better than the great Tolen.

TOLEN: That sexual incompetent.

COLIN: Eh?

NANCY: He's not incompetent. What's incompetent?

TOM: No good.

NANCY: No good? He's marvellous, he raped me.

TOLEN: You have not been raped.

NANCY: I have.

TOLEN: You have not been raped and you know it.

NANCY: He raped me.

TOLEN: You have not.

NANCY: I have.

TOLEN: And certainly not by——

NANCY: Rape.

TOLEN: Him. He wouldn't know one end of a woman from the other.

NANCY: Rape, rape.

TOLEN: The number of times I've seen him. "Has Cardiff got big docks?" He'll never make it never.

COLIN: What?

TOLEN: Granted——

COLIN: What did you say?

NANCY: He raped me.

TOLEN: Granted he might do better with help—and he needs help. Bow-legged, spavin-jointed, broken-winded, down and out. Look at him.

COLIN: Eh?

NANCY: He's rugged.

TOLEN: I ask you is it possible——?

NANCY: Handsome.

TOLEN: Or likely——?

NANCY: Marvellous, super.

TOLEN: It takes him four months hard labour to get a girl to bed.

NANCY: He did, you did, didn't you?

TOLEN: That oaf.

NANCY: Go on, tell him.

COLIN: Hard labour?

TOLEN: You keep out of this.

NANCY: Yes, you shut up.

TOLEN: A rapist, oh really.

NANCY: Rape. Rape.

TOLEN: That chicken.

NANCY: Rape.

TOLEN: How stupid can you get? Too ridiculous.

NANCY: Rape. Rape.

TOLEN: Probably impotent.

(TOM *begins to knock a nail into the wall about nine feet above floor level. His banging deliberately punctuates the following.*)

COLIN: Why not?

TOLEN: What?

COLIN: Why not me, pray?

NANCY: Rape. Rape.

COLIN : Why not me? (*To* TOM) Be quiet. (*To* TOLEN)
Sexually incompetent! Hard labour!
(NANCY *starts to chirrup round the room*, COLIN
while talking at the others follows after her.)

NANCY : Rape pape pape pape pape pape——
(TOM *is banging*.)

COLIN : (*to* TOM). Shut up. (*To* TOLEN) Now you
listen——

TOM : Rape!

NANCY : R e e e e e e ep.

COLIN : All, all I can say is out—out—outrage. Outrage.
Outrage. (*To* TOM) Shut up. (*To* TOLEN) Rape,
rape, didn't I? Couldn't I? I did—I mean I
could—(*to* TOM) Shut up. (*To* TOLEN) Now you
listen, now get this straight—(*to* TOM) Shut up.
(*To* TOLEN) I am not incapable!

NANCY : Pay pay pay pay pay pay pee pee pee pee pee
pee.

COLIN : (*to* NANCY). Really, I didn't, really, I wouldn't
mind—(*to* TOM) Shut up, be quiet. (*To* NANCY)
I'd love to—I mean. (*To* TOM) Shut up!
(NANCY *is now keeping up an almost permanent
yelp*. TOM *starts on another nail in another wall*.)
Shut up, shut up. Now get this, get this—get—
get—shut up—I could've yes. I could've if I'd
wanted—rape her—shut up—I didn't—you
think I couldn't—shut up—I—I—Shut! Shut!
I'll show you!
(COLIN *starts to chase* NANCY *round the room*.
TOM'*s banging covers the chase and stops at the
end of it*.)
Just let me—get her—I'll—I'll show you—I'll—
I'll—yes I'll—just you I'll show—oh—oh—oh—
oh—oh——

NANCY: Oh—oh—oh—oh——
(*A chase with objects.*)
COLIN: Oh—oh—oh—oh——
NANCY: Oh—oh—oh—oh——
TOLEN: You can't even catch her Colin, can you? Never mind rape her. I think you are quite incapable of making a woman, Colin. Look, I'll show you.
COLIN: If you touch her—
—I'll kill you!
(*Very long pause.* TOLEN *releases* NANCY *who goes to* COLIN. *A girl passes the window.* TOLEN *laughs gently and then exits through window.* TOM *hoists chair on to the nails in the wall.*)
TOM: Ah yes, beautiful.
(TOM *hoists second chair on to nails.*)
Ah, yes.
(*Exit* TOM.)

(*The End*)